CHILDREN
398.2
Y784pe

Yolen, Jane.
Pegasus, the flying horse /
EAST   1033786458

JUN 1 7 1999

D0382370

To
Fresno County Library

from

**The Friends
of the
Fresno County Library**

PEGASUS,
the Flying Horse

RETOLD BY JANE YOLEN

ILLUSTRATED BY LI MING

DUTTON CHILDREN'S BOOKS

New York

For Christine Crow—Corvina—thanks for the help.
—J.Y.

To an editor who cares about books and
artists who illustrate them.
—L.M.

Pegasus is available on audiocassette,
compact disc, and animated video from Lightyear Entertainment,
350 Fifth Avenue, Suite 5101, New York, New York 10118
Call 1-800-229-7867 for information

Text copyright © 1998 by Jane Yolen
Illustrations copyright © 1998 by Lightyear Entertainment, L.P.
All rights reserved
No part of this book may be reproduced in any form without permission in writing
from the Publisher

Library of Congress Cataloging-in-Publication Data
Yolen, Jane.
Pegasus, the flying horse / retold by Jane Yolen : illustrated by Li Ming.
p.   cm.
Summary: Retells how, with the help of the goddess Athena, the handsome and overly proud
Bellerophon tames the winged horse Pegasus and conquers the montrous Chimaera.
ISBN 0-525-65244-2
1. Pegasus (Greek mythology)—Juvenile literature. 2. Pegasus (Greek mythology) [1. Mythology,
Greek.]   I. Li Ming, 1958–   II. Title.   BL820.P4Y65   1998
396.2′0938′0454—dc21   97–39365   CIP   AC

Published in the United States by Dutton Children's Books,
a member of Penguin Putnam Inc.,
375 Hudson Street, New York, New York 10014

Designed by Mina Greenstein   Printed in Hong Kong
First Edition 10 9 8 7 6 5 4 3 2 1

AUTHOR'S NOTE

THE STORY OF BELLEROPHON, like many of the Greek hero tales, is the story of a flawed young man full of what the Greeks called *hubris*, or pride. In this case, Bellerophon unthinkingly causes his brother's death and never mourns the boy, believing himself as great as a god. The immortals who dwelt on Mount Olympus—the Greek version of heaven—never rewarded such men but rather punished them for their overweening pride.

Many of Bellerophon's adventures follow a familiar folktale pattern: the hero is set tasks likely to kill him and yet he accomplishes all with the aid of a magical helper, winning the king's daughter for his wife. Though this retelling only recounts Bellerophon's battle with the hideous Chimaera, he was actually set further tasks as well, including battles with the Amazons and with pirates.

The term "Bellerophonic letters" arose from this story, meaning any kind of communication that a person carries that contains information prejudicial to himself. The places—Corinth, Lycia (now Turkey), and Tiryns are all real.

Many early Greek poets wrote about the adventures of Bellerophon, most notably Homer in the *Iliad* and Horace in the *Odes*. The stories all differ slightly. Some say Bellerophon slept in Athena's temple before visiting King Proteus, some that he was granted the golden bridle only after fleeing to Lycia. There are differing descriptions of the Chimaera as well. But all the stories end in his unheroic death when he is punished for his *hubris* in wanting to join the gods on Mount Olympus. Homer wrote that Bellerophon was last heard of "wandering alone, eating his heart out, avoiding the paths of men."

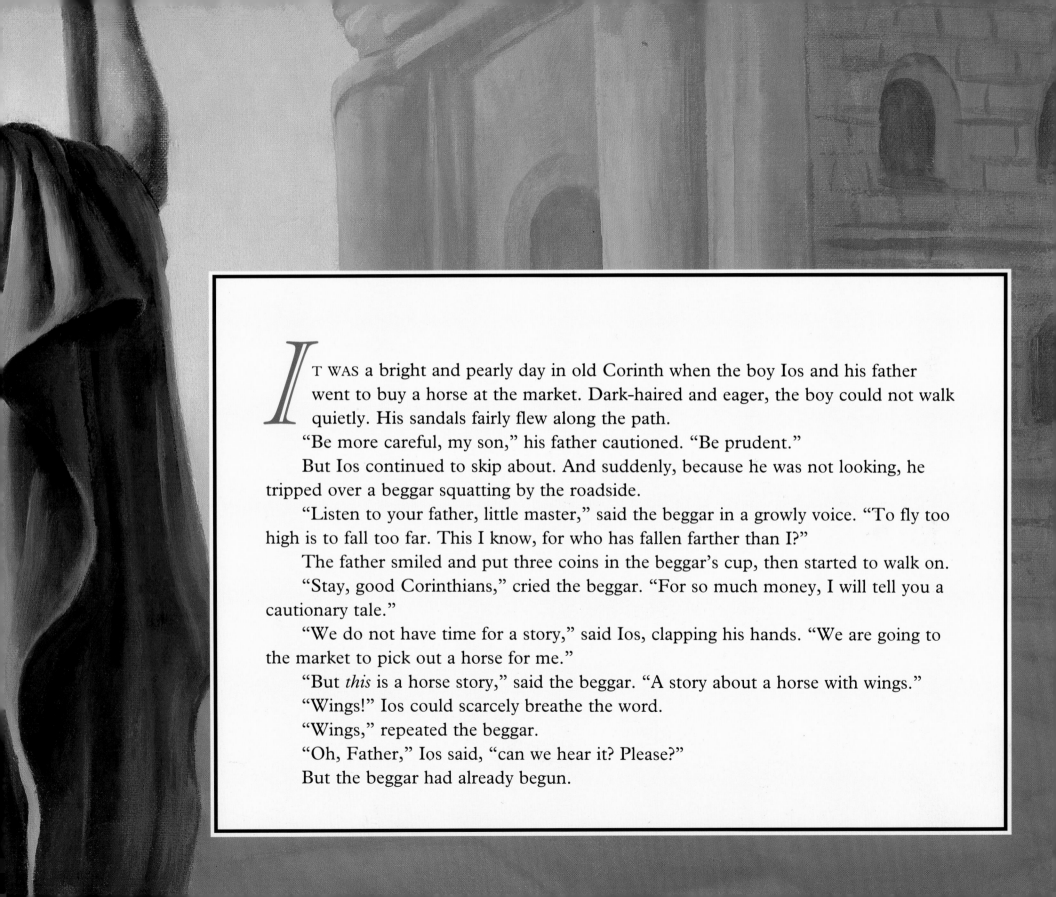

*I*T WAS a bright and pearly day in old Corinth when the boy Ios and his father went to buy a horse at the market. Dark-haired and eager, the boy could not walk quietly. His sandals fairly flew along the path.

"Be more careful, my son," his father cautioned. "Be prudent."

But Ios continued to skip about. And suddenly, because he was not looking, he tripped over a beggar squatting by the roadside.

"Listen to your father, little master," said the beggar in a growly voice. "To fly too high is to fall too far. This I know, for who has fallen farther than I?"

The father smiled and put three coins in the beggar's cup, then started to walk on.

"Stay, good Corinthians," cried the beggar. "For so much money, I will tell you a cautionary tale."

"We do not have time for a story," said Ios, clapping his hands. "We are going to the market to pick out a horse for me."

"But *this* is a horse story," said the beggar. "A story about a horse with wings."

"Wings!" Ios could scarcely breathe the word.

"Wings," repeated the beggar.

"Oh, Father," Ios said, "can we hear it? Please?"

But the beggar had already begun.

IN THE CITY OF CORINTH, many years ago—the beggar said—there lived a young man named Bellerophon. His hair was the blue-black of the deep ocean, his eyes the lighter blue-green of waves. Some said he was the son of King Glaucus, but more said he was Poseidon's own son—Poseidon, god of the sea.

The women of Corinth whispered and sighed whenever Bellerophon walked by, for he was very handsome. But he did not desire any of them. Nor did he desire gold or power. All he wanted was to ride the great winged horse, Pegasus, who—it was said— was to be found in a field outside of the city and guarded by the gods. Bellerophon had never seen the horse except in dreams. Still, the flying horse was all he desired.

Now Pegasus was clearly no ordinary horse. Above his broad white shoulders grew great wings, with alabaster feathers and vanes of gold.

And he had not been born in any ordinary way either. When the hero Perseus had slain the snake-haired gorgon, Medusa, her blood had rained down upon the ground. There earth and blood had combined to create the flying horse—Pegasus.

The goddess Athena herself had caught and tamed the horse. It was she who brought him to the field. But no one was allowed to come near him. He had never been ridden by a mortal.

All the young men in Corinth desired Pegasus, but none wanted him as much as Bellerophon. Bellerophon found he could not stop thinking about the winged horse. He could not sleep or eat for the wanting. He paced back and forth talking about the horse, forgetting his friends, ignoring his studies, dreaming only of Pegasus. It was as if he were possessed.

His mother watched him grow thin, watched him grow pale, watched the rings form under his sea-colored eyes. Fearing he would die of such a longing, she sent him to consult the wise man Polyidus for advice.

"Go to the temple of Athena," said Polyidus, "she who caught and tamed the horse. Put aside all thoughts, all desires. Go to the temple and sleep. Surely the goddess will speak to you in your dreams."

Bellerophon bade his mother good-bye, took a thin wool blanket that she had woven, and went to Athena's temple. It was a large building, with great white pillars and a floor of colored tiles.

When dusk came and all the other worshippers went home, Bellerophon alone stayed on. He spread his blanket near the goddess' altar, sat down, and closed his eyes. As night trembled around him, he fell asleep. He did not know he dreamed, but he dreamed.

He dreamed that Athena stood before him, something gold and shimmering in her hands, saying, "You are my brother Poseidon's true son. I will let you alone ride the winged horse. You will need my magic bridle. Take it." And then she was gone.

Bellerophon awoke and it was still night, yet the temple was lit by a strange light. There, on the temple floor, not far from the altar, was a golden bridle. When he touched it, his hand tingled; when he picked it up, the light vanished.

"Thank you, Athena," he whispered. Then he lay down on the blanket and fell asleep, the bridle clutched in his arms.

He had no more dreams.

In the morning, Bellerophon went to the field where Pegasus was pastured. Slowly he walked toward the horse, who seemed to be waiting for him. When at last he reached Pegasus, he touched the great white shoulder with a tentative hand. The horse did not even twitch.

"I am Bellerophon, son of Poseidon," he said, whispering his boast. "Will you let me bridle you?"

Pegasus shook his head, but only to rid himself of flies, and Bellerophon slipped the golden bridle over the horse's muzzle, up over his eyes, over the crown of his head.

"Now will you let me ride?" whispered Bellerophon. Without waiting for an answer, he leaped lightly onto the horse's back.

Startled, Pegasus pumped his mighty wings once, and flew up into the air. If Bellerophon had not been holding tight to the reins, had his legs not been wrapped tight around the horse's great barreled body, he would surely have fallen off.

Another great cleaving of the white wings, and they were above the field and the sea beyond, above trees, above the hills, above the far mountains, just under the plump clouds.

Cautiously, Bellerophon peered down. He saw how the land stretched out, now green fields, now gold. He saw how the waves in the water made runnels in the sea. He felt the cold wind on his arms, the rush of air making streamers of his dark hair. He knew he could never be happier.

"There is not much caution in that tale," said Ios' father.

"But a marvelous horse," Ios pointed out.

The beggar chuckled. "This is but the story's start."

"Then there's more?" Ios asked eagerly. "More of the horse?"

"More of the horse," the beggar said. "And more of Bellerophon, too."

Now that he could ride the flying horse—said the beggar—Bellerophon should have been completely happy. But he was a god's son. It was not in him to be content.

Because he took great pride in being allowed on Athena's horse, he grew selfish. When his young brother Deliades asked for a ride, Bellerophon laughed. "You have but a man for a father. My father is a god. You are too lowly to ride this horse." Roughly he pushed Deliades away.

It should not have happened, but it did. Deliades fell backwards, hit his head on a stone, and did not move.

Alarmed, Bellerophon left the boy where he lay. He leaped onto Pegasus' back and rode away into the sky.

As they went higher and higher, Bellerophon forgot the tragedy below. "I am a god's son!" he cried aloud. "I do what I will!" The wind removed all blame from his shoulders and he urged Pegasus even higher until they could see Corinth no more.

At last, Bellerophon reined in the flying horse, and they landed on the low-lying Argive Plain. He was certain King Proteus of Tiryns would welcome him and pardon any of his sins.

So, leading Pegasus, he found his way to the hilltop castle of the king. And because of the wondrous horse, and because of Bellerophon's own striking looks, the guards did not stop him, thinking him a god.

When he was taken into the spacious hall where the king held court, Bellerophon knelt down.

The king was pleased with him. "Rise, Bellerophon—boy or god—and eat at my table."

The queen echoed his sentiments, saying, "Yes. Yes. Feast with us."

So Bellerophon became the king's own guest, which meant a great deal more in those times than it does today.

Bellerophon stayed a guest in the palace for many weeks while Pegasus cropped the Tirynian grass outside the high stone walls.

Meanwhile, the queen had fallen in love with the handsome young man. She composed poems and songs about him. One evening, when she found him alone in a darkened room, she even tried to kiss him.

But Bellerophon turned his face from her, for he did not love her, any more than he had loved the women in Corinth. Besides, he was her husband's guest.

"You shall be sorry for this," the queen said in an angry voice. "No man dares treat me so." She left the room and went at once to her husband and told him a terrible lie.

"Your guest—the *boy* Bellerophon—took hold of me without my permission." She turned her head and pretended to weep.

King Proteus was furious. He wanted Bellerophon dead. But as Bellerophon was his guest, the king could not kill him outright, so he devised a cunning plan. He sent Bellerophon to his father-in-law, King Iobates, with a sealed letter that said: "Kill the bearer of this message at once. He has tried to violate my wife, your eldest daughter."

Bellerophon thought he was being sent on a special mission for the king and it made him very proud. He mounted Pegasus with much eagerness, the message tucked away in his shirt.

Once more the great wings cleaved the air, and horse and rider flew up into the sky.

Bellerophon thought he had never been happier.

"Now I know how the gods must feel!" he called out. If he felt the horse shudder beneath him, he thought it was only the wind.

The trip to Lycia, the land of King Iobates, was far away in Asia Minor. But Pegasus flew it in a single day. Again, when Bellerophon and his winged horse landed, he was greeted as if he were a god.

King Iobates himself took Bellerophon by the hands, saying, "Nine days we shall feast. Nine days we shall sing and dance." He refused to even read the sealed letter until the nine days were over.

When King Iobates finally read the message from Proteus, he was in a terrible quandry. Bellerophon was now his guest. Iobates had feasted him and fed him and given him one of the finest rooms in the palace. How could he possibly kill the boy?

Iobates worried about this for a full day, and then he had an idea. He called Bellerophon to him, saying, "You are surely a mighty hero, and a mighty hero is just what my poor country needs."

Bellerophon liked being called a hero, and so he did not hesitate. "Ask and I shall do it, sire. Whatever it is."

King Iobates smiled a crafty smile. "There is a great monster ruining the northern part of my land," he said. "It burns the crops and kills my people, and no one in Lycia has been able to slay it."

"What kind of monster?" Bellerophon asked.

"It is called the Chimaera," replied the king. "It has the front feet of a lion, the tail of a serpent, the body and hind feet of a goat. It breathes searing blasts of fire from its three heads."

"I will fight it," proclaimed Bellerophon. "And I will win."

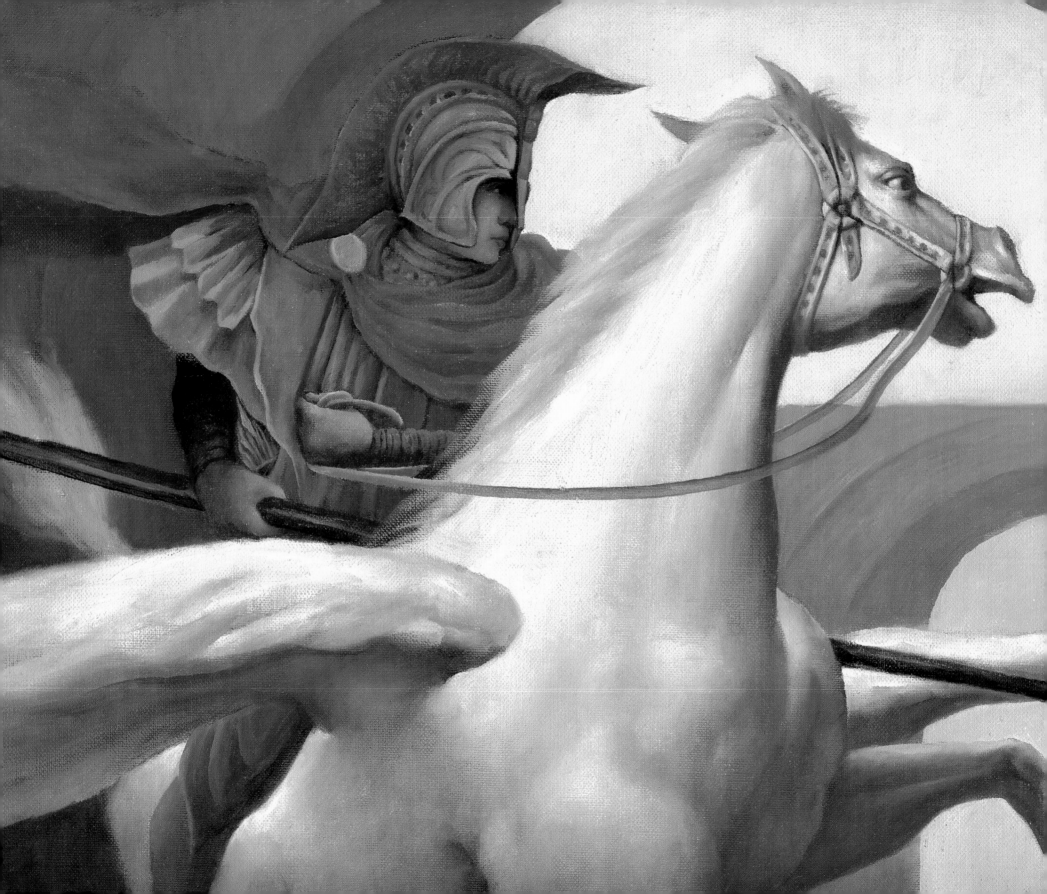

The king gave Bellerophon a suit of armor and a bow made of Lycian yew. He gave him a quiver of new arrows and a long steel-pointed spear.

Bellerophon took the armor and arrows and bow, but he was not entirely satisfied with the spear. He went to the armorer and said, "Remove the spear point and put instead a great ball of lead at the end of the shaft."

The armorer laughed. "A ball of lead will not pierce that monster's body."

But Bellerophon insisted and finally the armorer did as he was asked. So armed, Bellerophon mounted Pegasus and off they flew into the sky.

As always, once in the air Bellerophon felt as great as any god. He was fearless as they flew north. In minutes he saw a spiral of smoke rising above some fields.

"Down," he urged the horse, and Pegasus circled lower and lower to hover above the place where the smoke began.

There was the monster, hideous beyond belief. The lion head had a mouth ringed with sharp teeth. The goat head was bloated and soiled. The serpent head was long and slick. The Chimaera raked the ground with its lion claws in front, its goat hooves behind, leaving great scores in the earth. All the while it belched fire and spit out smoke.

For a moment Bellerophon was terrified. But the monster never looked up, and there was Bellerophon's one chance.

Carefully drawing his bow, he shot arrow after arrow down on the monster so quickly it was like a deadly rain. The Chimaera's goat body bled scorching blood, its serpent tail lashed in agony.

Only then did Bellerophon command the winged horse to land. The minute Pegasus touched the ground, Bellerophon leaped off and drove his spear, with its lead ball tip, into one of the wounded monster's open mouths.

The Chimaera's fiery breath melted the lead, and the molten metal ran down its throat, searing its heart. And so it died.

Remounting, Bellerophon returned to King Iobates, a hero indeed.

The Lycians greeted him with great celebrations. The women all sought his attention, but Bellerophon blushed and turned away.

When King Iobates saw how shy with women the young hero was, he began to wonder about his son-in-law's letter. He asked for Bellerophon's side of the story. And when he had heard it, King Iobates not only believed Bellerophon, but said, "Stay here and marry my youngest daughter. You shall be king after me. Lycia needs such a hero."

King Iobates' daughter was beautiful and modest. Bellerophon wed her gladly.

He had never been happier. And yet—he was a god's son. It was not in him to be content.

Bellerophon was a hero. He was to be a king. He had a flying horse. He was the son of a god. But he was not himself a god, and he could not sleep or eat for wanting to be one. He paced back and forth, forgetting his wife, forgetting his adopted land and friends. It was as if he were possessed.

His worried wife watched him grow thin and pale. And when he told her he would fly up to Mount Olympus to claim his place among the gods, she wept and begged him not to go. But Bellerophon was determined.

"I am my father's son," he said. "My place is by his side." He kissed his wife, bade farewell to his father-in-law, and mounted Pegasus. Away they flew, higher and higher into the air, past mountains, past eagles' aeries, past the swiftly moving clouds.

Zeus, the king of the gods, saw them coming. He knew what was in Bellerophon's heart. "Do not try to fly too high, boy," he shouted in a voice deep as thunder. "It is not meant for a mortal to become a god."

If Bellerophon heard, he did not listen. On Pegasus' back he already felt like a god. He urged the horse on.

So Zeus sent a gadfly to sting the winged horse. Pegasus kicked and bucked in the air, and Bellerophon could not hold on. Down and down and down he tumbled, down to earth where all the mortals dwelt.

His father, Poseidon, took pity on Bellerophon and did not let him die in the fall. But Bellerophon lay in a ditch for days, his legs cruelly broken. The right one never did heal properly, so he was unable to walk all the way back to Lycia. However, he did manage, through begging, to get to Corinth where he lived the rest of his life telling stories to passersby.

"What happened to the flying horse?" Ios asked in a hushed voice.

"Ah," said the beggar, "Pegasus stayed on at Mount Olympus with the gods, carrying Zeus' thunderbolts."

Ios did not speak for a moment, then looked at the beggar, eyes shining. "Is that a true story?"

"A story needn't be actual to be true," the old beggar said, standing. He winked one of his ocean wave-colored eyes, then walked away.

"Ready to go on to the market?" asked Ios' father.

"I am ready, Father," the boy said. "I want a horse now more than ever. But not, I think, one with wings."

"Little chance of that," his father replied, with a small smile. "The price for such a horse is more than I want to pay."

"Or I," agreed Ios. And he turned to stare at the beggar, who was limping down the road, his right leg dragging badly behind.

1033786458